For Priscilla and Jack Moulton

Houghton Mifflin/Clarion Books
52 Vanderbilt Avenue, New York, NY 10017

Text copyright © 1980 by Carol Carrick
Illustrations copyright © 1980 by Donald Carrick

Library of Congress Cataloging in Publication Data

Carrick, Carol.   The climb.
Summary: Brendan is scared when he and his older cousin
begin to climb the mountain, but on the way down,
it's Nora who becomes frightened.
[1. Fear—Fiction. 2. Cousins—Fiction]
I. Carrick, Donald. II. Title.
PZ7.C2344Cm   [E]   80-12965   ISBN 0-395-29431-2

THE CLIMB

BY CAROL CARRICK
PICTURES BY DONALD CARRICK

Houghton Mifflin/Clarion Books/New York

The sign was marked BEGINNERS' TRAIL.

"Are we going up there?" Brendan asked, squinting at the mountain that rose above the forest ahead. At the top was a great brow of rock, sprinkled with dark, stunted trees.

His cousin Nora nodded.

"Not me," said Brendan. "I don't want to."

"Don't be scared. It's easy," Nora coaxed. "See, the sign says it's for beginners. People go up all the time. It's really great!"

"I'm not scared," Brendan mumbled, looking at his feet. "I just don't want to."

"What a baby," Nora said to herself. Brendan was four years younger than Nora but she thought he acted even younger. He had come with Aunt Barbara for the weekend and Nora was supposed to entertain him.

Nora had wanted to rock on the cool farmhouse porch and listen to the women talk. Instead, Mother had packed a lunch and told her to take her cousin on a picnic.

"Come on, Bren, we'll just climb a little way up and then we'll have lunch," Nora said.

Waves of heat pressed against them as they walked through the field, and grasshoppers shot across their path like sparks.

"I'm so sweaty," Brendan whined. "And I'm thirsty." He eyed the thermos sticking out of Nora's pack.

"But we just started," Nora said with annoyance.

When they entered the cool, damp forest Brendan stopped complaining. Its silence seemed to work a spell on him.

"You can be the trail guide," Nora said so Brendan would feel important.

He ran ahead to discover each rock and tree that was marked with red paint until he came to the solid wall of the mountain that rose almost straight up. He turned and looked at Nora.

"Just follow the red markers," Nora said.

Tree roots formed natural steps up the huge boulders piled along the base of the mountain. As the trail grew steep the children clung to the trees. The path was spongy with fallen needles.

"It smells like Christmas," Brendan said.

Then there was nothing ahead but the broad brow of pitted grey rock that they had seen near the top of the mountain. There were no footholds and nothing to grab onto.

"What do we do now?" Brendan asked.

Nora grinned. Without answering she walked right up the slope, and then turned back.

"See, it's easy."

"You said we would stop if I wanted to," Brendan whimpered. "I want to go home now."

"Okay. Go home, baby," Nora taunted. "But I'm having the picnic. We're almost there."

Brendan hesitated and then started slowly, cautiously up the rock. "Faster. You've got to walk faster," Nora urged. "Don't stop!"

But Brendan wavered. His breath was coming in hoarse gasps. He felt the pull backwards and almost lost his balance. He dropped to his hands and knees a few yards from where Nora waited.

"Nora!" Brendan pleaded. "Help me!"

He pressed his face to the rough stone and looked down to the valley below. It began to roll before his eyes, making him feel sick.

"Nora, I'm going to fall! I'm afraid!"

"Don't look down, Brendan. Look at me."

Nora held out her hand to Brendan. She could see he was really frightened.

"Look at me, Brendan," she said firmly. "You're not going to fall. You're going to walk up as easy as pie."

Slowly Brendan crawled up, his eyes never leaving Nora's outstretched hand. When he reached her she pulled him to his feet. From there on the slope was more gradual and together they walked the short distance to the top. Brendan laughed nervously as he felt how well his rubber soles gripped the rock.

Nora sat down and laid out the picnic.

"Look, Nora," Brendan pointed. "There's your house. I wonder if they can see us up here."

Below them in the valley, Nora's house, the barn, the trees and even the cows in their bright field looked like tiny toys. Behind the valley marched row after row of mountains, each looking as if it were

cut from cardboard. Those farthest away grew fainter and fainter, until the last ones dissolved into the sky.

Nora and Brendan ate their lunch. Then they stretched out lazily on the warm rock and watched a distant hawk rise screeching on the updrafts of air.

Nora stuffed the lunch wrappers in her sack and stood up. "I've got something else to show you, Brendan."

A red arrow on the rock pointed to a wooded path that wound around the top of the mountain. The trees here grew slowly and were twisted by the wind. The trail soon crossed over a small cave formed by a rock slab balanced on several others.

Brendan had to bend down to peer inside. "Does anything live in there?" he asked.

"Bears, probably," Nora answered.

Brendan jumped back

"Don't worry," Nora said. "They sleep during the day."

"Is this what you wanted to show me?" Brendan asked.

"No. There's something even better," Nora said. "Come on."

The shadowy path snaked around and between more boulders, but the hard climbing part was over. After a while the forest opened on all sides to blue sky and their trail ended again upon bare rock. Nora steadied Brendan as he followed the last arrow up to the topmost jut of rock.

"Boy!" Brendan shouted. "This must be the top of the world!"

It was not their familiar world of houses and small farms that was mirrored in the lake below them. It was a world of low mountains furred with trees like the backs of sleeping animals.

"Didn't I tell you it was great?" Nora asked.

But Brendan ignored her question.

"Don't you wish you could ride on those shadows?" he asked. He was watching the shadows cast by the clouds slide across the slopes like magic carpets.

On the way back Brendan forgot his fear of the mountain. Every time Nora pointed out one of the trail markers he would look annoyed and say, "I saw it already." And if she tried to help him over a difficult place he would brush her aside, saying confidently, "I can do it myself."

Nora decided to play a joke on him.

"Hey Bren," she said with excitement as she perched on a tree that had fallen across the path. "I've got a great idea for a game. I'll go ahead to the big rock where we ate lunch and wait for you. Pretend that I'm lost. You be the search party and find me. Okay?" She tried hard not to smile and make him suspicious.

Brendan's face lit up. "Yeah! I'll count up to fifty and then I'll come find you," he agreed.

He turned his back on her and covered his eyes, counting aloud, "One, two, three, four . . ."

Nora raced ahead until she came to the cave. It was smaller than she remembered. Maybe there *is* something in there, she thought. But she couldn't waste time wondering. Brendan's footsteps were already thudding down the path. He couldn't have counted to fifty.

When she scrambled inside on her hands and knees, she found it wasn't really a cave. It was a rock tunnel with straight sides almost as narrow as her body, like the Egyptian tomb she had seen at the museum. The ceiling became so low that she had to wriggle along on her elbows, pushing at the soft dirt floor with her toes. Brendan's footsteps were overhead now. She squeezed back as far as she could so he wouldn't be able to see her.

She tried an experimental growl. "Rrrrah!"

It echoed from the rock walls.

"Grrraah!" she growled louder, enjoying how deep her voice sounded.

"Grrrah, Rrrahrrah!" she added for good measure and bit her lip to keep from laughing.

She listened. Everything was quiet. She could imagine Brendan running for dear life. She laughed out loud.

Then she was aware of the moldy odor in the cave. It smelled of earth and rotting wood, like the crawl space under the house where creepy things scurried. She couldn't see very well now because her body blocked most of the light coming in from the entrance.

Maybe I'd better go after Brendan, she thought. He'll tell Mother on me. Or maybe he's lost the trail.

She straightened her arms to back out, banging her head hard against the roof of the cave. "Ow!" She lowered her shoulders, but as she bent her knees to crawl, the rough stone scraped the skin over her backbone where her shirt had ridden up. She couldn't get out!

Nora stopped for a minute to think. How had she gotten in? Then something cold touched her bare ankle. Nora screamed in surprise. She turned her head to see what it was and hit her forehead. Tears sprang to her eyes.

Nora was afraid to move her leg, afraid she might touch that cold something again. She shuddered and inched forward a bit in the darkness.

Something brushed her face. She pushed it away. A spider web. It must be a big one. Where was the spider? Was it in her hair? It must be in her hair. But she couldn't reach that far. Frantically she thrashed her head and shoulders, but with each move she struck the icy rock.

Nora was panting now like a frightened animal.

"I've got to get out!" she yelled. "I want to go home!"

Brendan had said the same thing when he was afraid of falling. He must be waiting for her on the rock, Nora thought. Or maybe he had started home without her. She groaned. Brendan didn't even know where she was.

"Brendan," she pleaded out loud. "Oh Brendan, *please* come back!"

"Nora? Are you in the cave, Nora?" a small voice asked. "What's the matter?"

Nora started. Had she really heard it, Brendan's voice? And so near!

"Brendan! I can't get out of here," Nora called.

"Did you get stuck?" he asked. "I can see your feet."

If Brendan could see her she couldn't be far from the outside. She could get out if she tried. Nora didn't feel alone any more, cut off from the rest of the world. The world was close, as close as Brendan's voice.

Slowly, awkwardly she wriggled out the way she had come in. It was much harder going backwards, but she was calm now, and she knew she could do it.

"Boy, you're all dirty," Brendan observed as she stood up and brushed herself off. "And you hurt your face!" The concern on *his* face made Nora feel ashamed.

"I'm sorry if I scared you when I growled," she said.

"That's okay," he answered. "You didn't scare me. I knew it was you all the time."

The climb down went quickly. They felt as if the earth were pulling them toward the bottom of the mountain and the muscles in their legs trembled from the strain. Brendan said nothing when they reached the bare rock face, but he placed his feet carefully and clung tightly to Nora's hand.

Soon they were on the almost flat part of the trail through the forest. Brendan was chattering happily now, and Nora pointed out the woodpecker's tree and a squirrel's nest.

Suddenly there was a loud squeal behind them. They both screamed. As Nora turned to look, there was another, smaller squeak.

"Oh!" She laughed with relief. "See that tree leaning against the other one? When the wind moves them, their bark rubs together. Did that scare you?"

"At first," Brendan admitted.

"It scared me, too," said Nora.

Brendan waited until they were out of the forest and walking across the field to ask, "Nora, could we go up the mountain again tomorrow?"

"Sure," Nora answered, giving her cousin a squeeze. "Only this time *you* hide, and I'll look for *you*."

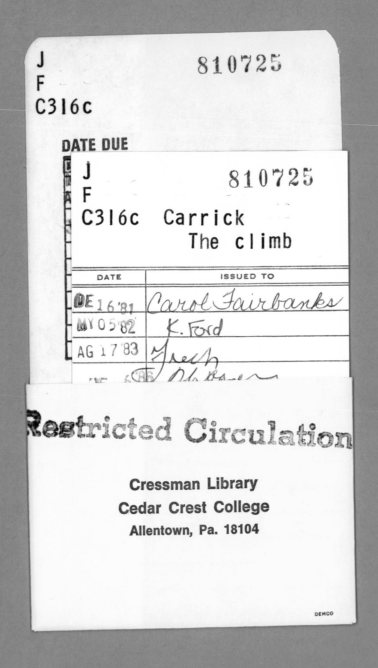